Relevé (rel-uh-VAY)

One

Two

Three

Tallulah's Solo

by MARILYN SINGER

Illustrations by
ALEXANDRA BOIGER

CLARION BOOKS

Houghton Mifflin Harcourt | Boston | New York | 2012

Clarion Books
215 Park Avenue South, New York, New York 10003

Clarion Books is an imprint of Houghton Mifflin Harcourt Publishing Company.
www.hmhbooks.com

The text was set in Pastonchi MT Std.
The illustrations were executed in watercolor, as well as watercolor mixed
with gouache and egg yolk, on Fabriano watercolor paper.

Library of Congress Cataloging-in-Publication Data
Singer, Marilyn.
Tallulah's solo / by Marilyn Singer ; illustrated by Alexandra Boiger.
p. cm.
Summary: Tallulah strives for perfection during ballet class and dreams of dancing
a solo in the upcoming recital, but her little brother, Beckett, who misbehaves
all during class, gets a better role than she does.
ISBN 978-0-547-33004-4
[1. Ballet dancing—Fiction. 2. Brothers
and sisters—Fiction.] I. Boiger, Alexandra,
ill. II. Title.
PZ7.S6172Taj 2012
[E]—dc23

2011025729

Manufactured in China
LEO 10 9 8 7 6 5 4 3 2 1
4500334906

To ballet dancers Lucy and Chaz
—M.S.

To Kathy, Mike, and Simone, with love
—A.B.

TALLULAH knew she was an
excellent ballet dancer. So she was
certain that this year she would be
doing a solo in the winter recital.

She was sure her little brother, Beckett, would become an excellent ballet dancer, too. She was glad he wanted to learn ballet. She could picture him, back straight, arms graceful, dancing behind her with the other kids while she did her perfect solo.

On the first day of dance school, Tallulah showed Beckett all around the studio. "This is the barre," she told him. "You hold on to balance."

"These are the mirrors so you can watch yourself move."

"And this is the chair where you sit if you misbehave."

"Uh-huh, uh-huh," said Beckett, but soon
he was more interested in sliding on the smooth
floor in his new black slippers.

Throughout his class, he paid attention only some of the time. He held first position for just a few seconds before kicking his feet from side to side.

He giggled when the teacher said, "Show me beautiful arms."

He picked his nose.

Tallulah couldn't believe that he wasn't sent to the time-out chair. At the end of his class, she told him, "Beckett, you have to pay better attention if you want to be a good dancer."

"Watch *me*."

"Uh-huh, uh-huh," said Beckett, and he did—for a little while. Then he wandered into the waiting room to play with his toy car.

"Very nice relevé, Tallulah," her teacher said when she rose and held her balance for a long time.

I will stay up even longer during my solo, she thought with a smile. I will look like a princess in my new tutu and sparkling tiara, and I'll dance like one, too.

But she wasn't sure Beckett
would be dancing behind her.
I hope he'll do better
next time, she told herself.

But next time, he kept making faces in the mirror.

And the following week, he tried to hang upside down on the barre.

That day he did end up in the time-out chair.
"Serves you right," Tallulah whispered. She *never*
fooled around during ballet.

Tallulah concentrated especially hard in her class.
"Lovely plié," said her teacher.

The plié I do during my solo will be even lovelier. The audience won't stop applauding. I will have to take five bows.

Then came the recital audition. A tall, slender man stood in the studio that Saturday afternoon. His name was Mr. Fontaine, and he was a choreographer. He told everyone he had created a new ballet called *The Frog Prince* and explained that he would be picking the dancers for it.

"The Frog Prince! Isn't that exciting?" Tallulah whispered to Beckett. She just *knew* Mr. Fontaine would choose her to be the princess. She wouldn't even mind kissing the frog!

The audience
will throw flowers,
she said to herself.
Real ones.
And Mr. Fontaine
will hand me the
biggest bouquet.

"Uh-huh, uh-huh." Beckett grinned and jumped
from one foot to the other, until his shoe fell off and
he had to put it back on.

Tallulah shook her head. She hoped that he would
at least get to be a water lily in the frog's pond.

Mr. Fontaine showed them steps and had them dance alone and in groups. Tallulah jumped lightly as a cat in a first-rate pas de chat, landed beautifully, and gave the choreographer her most excellent royal smile.

On Monday she was still smiling when she and Beckett and their mother arrived at the ballet studio. The list was already on the bulletin board. Tallulah ran over to find her name next to "Princess."

But it wasn't there.

"Look, Tallulah," said her mother. "You're one of the princess's ladies-in-waiting! And Beckett, you're the frog before he turns into the prince!"

"Ribbit!" croaked Beckett, hopping around the hall.

"The frog! That's not fair!" Tallulah cried. "He got a big part even though he goofs off. I got a little part, and I work so hard!"

She ran into the girls' room and threw down her ballet bag so hard that it banged into the garbage can. "*The Frog Prince* is a stupid story, and Beckett's going to be a stupid frog!" she yelled. She stayed in the girls' room until Beckett's class was over.

She did not talk to him when her class began.

During rehearsals she did not look at him while he learned his duet with the princess. Mr. Fontaine and their teacher were paying ENOUGH attention to him. Before long the whole audience will pay attention. Nobody will notice me at all. Nobody will throw a single flower. Tallulah scowled.

Then one afternoon, her mother said, "I think Beckett could use your help."

Tallulah sniffed. "Frogs don't need any help."

"Our frog does," her mother replied. "You know he decided to take ballet because of you."

Tallulah sniffed again.

Then she sighed and went to find her brother. He was in his room, staring in the mirror, trying to stay down in a grand plié. "I'll never do this right," he cried.

Suddenly, Tallulah remembered all the times he used to watch her practice in her mirror, then try out the moves on his own. He really did decide to take ballet because of me.

Standing as straight as their teacher, she said
firmly, "Yes, you will. Now, watch me."

This time Beckett paid close attention.
She showed him how to do his other steps
as well.

By the recital, Tallulah was the most graceful of the ladies-in-waiting, and Beckett had become a pretty good frog.

Mr. Fontaine told him what an excellent job he'd done. "It's because Tallulah helped me," Beckett explained.

"I see," said the choreographer. "I'll remember that."

And he did. That spring when he returned to choreograph the year-end recital, he picked Tallulah and Beckett to star in his latest ballet, *Hansel and Gretel*. In the grand finale, Tallulah, flashing her best big-sister smile, rescued her brother from the wicked witch. And as they spun around the stage, the audience applauded their perfect duet.

Plié (plee-AY)

One

Two

Three